Once Upon a Rhinoceros

Written by Avril van der Merwe

Illustrated by Heidi-Kate Greeff

DEDICATION

This book is dedicated to the wildlife rangers
who spend their lives working tirelessly for the
protection and preservation of our wildlife.
We are eternally grateful.

Once, upon a rhinoceros, grew a most magnificent horn. This horn was very long and shaped in a perfect arc that ended in the sharpest of points.

Rhinoceros used her horn to protect her baby and keep him safe from dangers. She used it to scratch for roots and small plants to eat. She used it to dig under the earth for water when the rains had stayed away too long. She used it to guide her baby as they browsed through the bush so that he would not get lost or fall into a donga.

All the animals respected Rhinoceros' horn.

When she walked through the bush, they would stop what they were doing to admire this majestic sight. Only one animal turned her back when she saw Rhinoceros coming. That animal was Hippopotamus.

Hippopotamus was jealous of Rhinoceros' horn. So jealous that she could not even bear to look at Rhino. When Rhinoceros came to the river to drink, Hippopotamus would sink under the water and blow loud air bubbles to show how annoyed she was.

What Hippopotamus wanted, more than anything, was a horn of her own.

Every day Hippo concentrated hard and squeezed with all her might, hoping she could make a horn grow out of her snout. Every day she crossed her eyes and looked at her nose to see whether a horn had started growing yet. Every day she was disappointed to see that her nose looked just the same as it had the day before.

One day Hippo decided that she needed another plan.

Hippo waited for the hottest part of the day, when Rhino was fast asleep under a tree. She tiptoed softly through the long grass until she was standing right in front of Rhinoceros who was curled up with her baby. For a moment Hippo stood as still as a rock, to make sure that Rhino did not wake up. Then she opened her huge jaws wide. In one snap, she snatched Rhino's horn, spun around, and raced away with it.

Behind her she heard an angry bellow, but Hippo did not stop. Instead she ran and ran until she reached her river. With a mighty splash she belly-flopped into the water and swam as fast as she could, all the way to the other side. Now at last she was safe and could enjoy her new horn all to herself.

First she had to put the horn on. Carefully she packed mud onto her snout. Then she cemented the horn into the mud pack and lay basking in the sun until it was baked dry. Hippo crossed her eyes to admire her new horn. It did not look as grand as she thought it should, but perhaps she needed time to get used to it.

Hippo was hungry after all this work. She decided to take a few nibbles of the long grass before she returned to the river. But as she swung around to make her way into the bush, the horn stabbed into a nearby tree trunk. Try as she might, she could not pull it out. She was stuck.

From the branches above her head, came a bark of laughter. A voice called out, "What are you doing with that horn, Hippo?"

"It's my new horn!" roared Hippo,
"Help me get it out of the tree, Baboon!"

"Ha, ha, ha!" barked Baboon, "You've got the horn on
backwards, Hippo! No wonder you are stuck in the tree!"

Hippo felt silly. "Well just help me get it out, will you?"
she grunted, "Then I'll put in on the right way around."

Baboon and his troop scampered down the tree.

One of them took hold of Hippo's stubby little tail.

Two of them grabbed the horn. The others gripped Hippo's legs.

Hippo and the baboons tugged
and pulled with all their might until,
finally, the horn popped out like a cork.

"A rhinoceros horn belongs on Rhinoceros, Hippo, not on you!"
scolded Baboon, "I think you should give it back."

"It's my horn now," snapped Hippopotamus, "Mind your own business."

Once again she packed mud on her snout, anchored the horn there – the right
way this time – and waited in the sun for it to dry. Once again she
crossed her eyes so she could see her horn. Now that it was on
the right way around, she thought it looked very good!

Hippo could not wait for all the animals to admire her new horn. She decided to swim back to her side of the river. It was almost time for the other animals to come down to the water for their sunset drink.

Hippo plunged into the water, but she had forgotten that her head was now heavier with a horn on it. Instead of swimming, she found herself upside down, with the horn stuck in the mud, and her bottom up in the air. Hippo wiggled and jiggled, and blew huge air bubbles, but could not free the horn from the mud.

Crocodile noticed the commotion
and came gliding along to find out what
all the fuss was about. When he saw Hippo
upside down with her face in the mud and her tail in the air,
he grinned an enormous grin. It was the funniest sight he had ever seen.

Crocodile sank under the water and saw
Hippo's eyes nearly popping out as she
tried to free herself. Crocodile was not
always kind, but he decided to help her.

He rolled and pushed with his powerful body until, with a slosh and a gurgle, the horn plopped free of the mud and Hippo's head bounced to the surface.

"You look silly with that horn, Hippo!" sneered Crocodile.

"It's my new horn," boasted Hippo.

"Well a rhino horn belongs on Rhinoceros, not on you!" snapped Crocodile.

"It's my horn now," retorted Hippopotamus, "Mind your own business!"

Hippo began to swim across the river, to where the animals had all gathered for their evening drink. She was careful to hold her head above the water, even though her neck was beginning to ache with the effort.

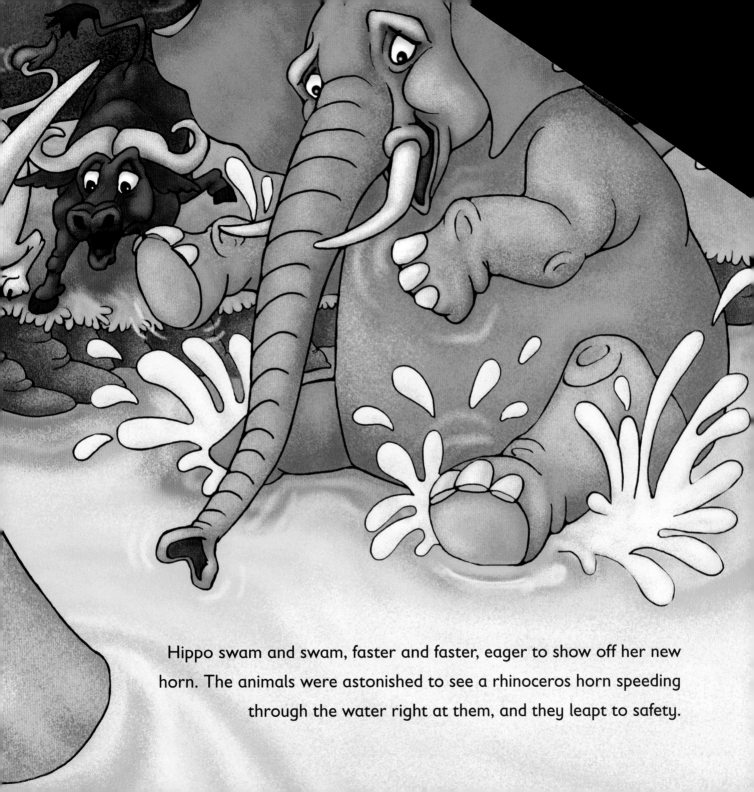

Hippo swam and swam, faster and faster, eager to show off her new horn. The animals were astonished to see a rhinoceros horn speeding through the water right at them, and they leapt to safety.

Hippo could not stop. She slammed headfirst into the river bank. Once again the horn got stuck in the mud! Her tail was up in the air and her stumpy back legs were waving around helplessly.

The animals began to laugh. They laughed and laughed, and then they laughed some more.

"Mmmmmph!" said Hippo, her mouth full of mud, "Mmmmmmph!"

Elephant felt sorry for Hippo. He stepped forward, wrapped his trunk around Hippo's middle, and set her back on her four feet.

"What are you doing with that horn, Hippopotamus?" he asked sternly.

"It's my new horn," sulked Hippo.

"It's not your horn at all," rumbled Elephant, "It belongs to Rhinoceros. A rhino horn does not belong anywhere else but on Rhinoceros."

Hippopotamus opened her mouth to tell Elephant to mind his own business. Instead, as she took a breath, she felt a huge yawn beginning. How tired she was from all her hard work! Her yawn grew bigger, until her huge mouth stretched as far as it could go, showing her enormous teeth. As the yawn grew and grew, her head tilted upwards. All of a sudden she felt a sharp pain in the middle of her back. She had stabbed herself with the horn!

Hippo snapped her mouth shut, then opened it wide again.

She let out a roar of pain as she stabbed herself in the back a second time.

"It serves you right, Hippopotamus," lectured Lion, "That horn does not belong to you. It belongs on Rhinoceros."

The animals heard a rustle in the grass behind them. They turned to see
Rhinoceros approaching slowly, her head, with its missing horn, drooping sadly.
The animals fell silent as they stepped aside to allow Rhinoceros through,
her baby trailing alongside her.

Rhinoceros stopped in front of Hippopotamus. She did not say anything. She simply stared at Hippopotamus and the horn on her snout. She stared and stared until Hippopotamus hung her head and looked away.

"I'm sorry, Rhinoceros. The horn belongs to you. I'll give it back."

The animals nodded in encouragement. "Rhino's horn belongs on Rhinoceros and nowhere else," they agreed.

Baboon and his troop scrambled down to the water. In a flash they whisked the horn off Hippopotamus and put it back on Rhinoceros.

Rhinoceros lifted her head high, her horn slicing through the air like a sickle. Her baby trotted around in front of her, happy that his Mama looked like herself again. The other animals gazed in admiration at Rhinoceros and her magnificent horn.

This time Hippopotamus did not turn her back on Rhinoceros.
She did not hide under the water and blow noisy bubbles. Instead
she joined the other animals in admiring Rhino's horn.

At last Rhinoceros spoke. "A rhinoceros horn belongs on a rhinoceros like a hippopotamus belongs in the water. Hippo, you don't have a horn and I cannot swim. A horn does not suit you, and swimming does not suit me. You admire my horn, and I admire your swimming. But we should not be jealous of each other."

Hippopotamus smiled her wide smile. She was pleased to hear that Rhinoceros admired her swimming. She slipped softly away into the deep water.

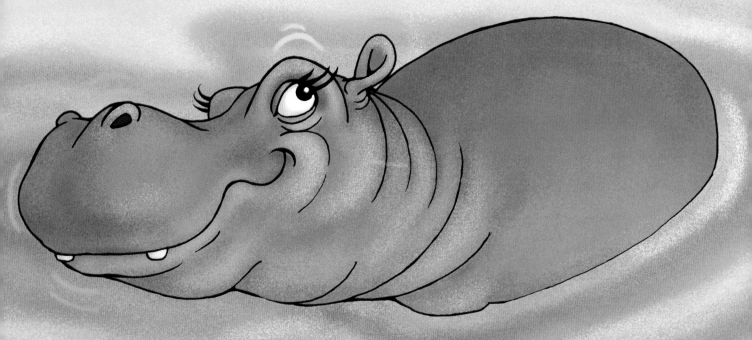

Rhinoceros stepped down to the river. The other animals followed. Together they enjoyed their sunset drink, while the reflection of Rhinoceros' magnificent horn rippled quietly in the water.

Avril van der Merwe, the author of *How Cheetah Got His Tears* and several prize-winning children's stories set in Africa, developed her love of writing for children while working as a pre-primary school teacher in Cape Town and a high-school English teacher in Johannesburg. Now living in the USA, she continues to write stories for children, and is also an inspirational speaker and writer.

Heidi-Kate Greeff loves creating and drawing animal characters that capture our hearts. She is constantly inspired by the endless supply of beauty, humour and adventure in the world. This is her second collaboration with Avril van der Merwe.

Published in 2018 by Puffin Books
an imprint of Penguin Random House South Africa (Pty) Ltd
Company Reg. No. 1953/000441/07
The Estuaries, 4 Oxbow Crescent, Century Avenue,
Century City 7441, Cape Town, South Africa
PO Box 1144, Cape Town, 8000, South Africa
www.penguinrandomhouse.co.za

PUBLISHER: Linda de Villiers
MANAGING EDITOR: Cecilia Barfield
DESIGN MANAGER: Beverley Dodd
DESIGNER: Helen Henn
EDITOR: Gill Gordon
Reproduction by Hirt & Carter Cape (Pty) Ltd
Printed and bound in India by Replika Press Pvt. Ltd.

ISBN 978-1-48590-037-5

MIX
Paper from responsible sources
FSC® C016779

This book is printed on FSC®-certified paper. Forest Stewardship Council® (FSC®) is an independent international non-governmental organization. Its aim is to support environmentally sustainable, socially and economically responsible global forest management.